# I WANT ANSWERS
# AND A PARACHUTE

Dear Jason + Matt —

Hi!

in

and
the dog
We can't
wait to
see you!

Love, Dad

# I WANT ANSWERS
# AND A PARACHUTE

## P.J. PETERSEN
## ILLUSTRATED BY ANNA DIVITO

SIMON & SCHUSTER BOOKS FOR YOUNG READERS
Published by Simon & Schuster
New York   London   Toronto   Sydney   Tokyo   Singapore

SIMON & SCHUSTER BOOKS FOR YOUNG READERS
Simon & Schuster Building, Rockefeller Center
1230 Avenue of the Americas, New York, New York 10020
Text copyright © 1993 by P.J. Petersen
Illustrations copyright © 1993 by Anna DiVito
SIMON & SCHUSTER BOOKS FOR YOUNG READERS
is a trademark of Simon & Schuster.
Designed by Vicki Kalajian
The text for this book is set in 14 pt. Simoncini Garamond.
Manufactured in the United States of America

10   9   8   7   6   5   4   3   2   1

*Library of Congress Cataloging-in-Publication Data*
Petersen, P.J.
I want answers and a parachute / by P.J. Petersen :
illustrated by Anna DiVito.
p.    cm.
Summary: Matt finds his little brother's fear
very annoying when they travel from Tucson
to San Francisco to visit their divorced father.
[1. Brothers—Fiction. 2. Fathers and sons—Fiction.
3. Divorce—Fiction. 4. Fear—Fiction.]
I. DiVito, Anna, ill. II. Title.   PZ7.P44197Iag
1993   [Fic.]—dc20   92-38262   CIP
ISBN: 0-671-86577-3

*For my friend Dick Dalrymple*
P.J.P.

*For Tracy and Mark Halliday*
A.D.

# I WANT ANSWERS AND A PARACHUTE

# CHAPTER ONE

We got to the airport early. But Mom was sure we were late. She grabbed a bag in each hand and ran across the parking lot.

"I can carry my own bag," I called. But she kept going. My little brother, Jason, and I raced after her.

"Will they give us parachutes?" Jason asked me.

"Hurry up," I said.

Jason stopped. "I want an answer. Will they give us parachutes?"

"No," I said. "Come on."

He started to run again. "What if we have to jump out? How can we jump without a parachute?"

"We won't have to jump out," I said.

"How do you know?"

"I've been on lots of plane trips," I said. I had been on two. But two is a lot.

Mom was fifty feet ahead by then. "Jason and Matt," she shouted. "Quit playing around."

"What if the plane catches on fire?" Jason asked.

"The plane is metal," I said. "It can't catch on fire."

"I'm still going to ask for a parachute," Jason said. "Just in case."

This was Jason's first airplane trip. We were going to visit our dad in San Francisco. Dad and Mom are divorced.

Jason and I live in Tucson, Arizona. After the divorce Dad lived about three miles from us. He came to all my soccer games. And Jason and I stayed at his place on weekends. That was great.

Then Dad had to move to San Francisco. And he came to see us once a month. That wasn't so good. But it was okay.

Now things were changing again. Dad had just married a woman named Ann. Jason and I were going to meet his new family on Presidents' Day weekend.

It was funny to think Dad had a new family. That made Jason and me the old family. That sounded bad. Like old shoes or an old car. Something you didn't need anymore.

I wanted this first visit to be great. Then maybe Dad would want us to come back again. But I was afraid Jason would mess things up.

I knew what Dad's new family looked like. He had sent a picture of him and Ann and her little girl, Cathy, and their dog, Ben. They all had big smiles. Even the dog.

When Jason saw the picture, he said, "Wow! I can't wait to see 'em."

Don't get the wrong idea. He didn't want a new sister or a stepmother. Especially not a stepmother. His first-grade class had just done a puppet show of *Cinderella*. He thought all stepmothers were like the one in that story.

But he was dying to see the dog. He's been begging Mom for years to get him a dog. Last year he bought a chain at a garage sale. He said he could use it to take our dog for a walk. If Mom ever bought one. (She didn't.) He tried to use the chain with our old cat, Millie. But she yowled until he took it off.

Jason wanted to take the chain to San Francisco. But Mom said no. So he tried to sneak it into his bag. Mom found it and took it out. Two times.

Finally we were inside the building. We stood in line at the counter. "Mom," Jason asked, "can planes catch on fire?"

Everybody in line looked at us. Some of them laughed. I hate that. People laugh at you because you're a dumb kid. And you look at your feet and feel stupid.

"Everything's going to be fine," she told him.

"I want an answer," Jason said.

"Quit yelling," I said. "I already gave you an answer."

The man at the counter set our bags on the moving belt. Then he stapled our tags to the ticket envelope. "You'll leave from Gate Three."

"I want a parachute," Jason told the man. "Please."

The man smiled. "Is this your first flight?"

"Yes. And I want a parachute."

"There's nothing to worry about," the man said.

"I want a parachute," Jason said again. But the man was taking the next person's ticket.

Mom handed me the ticket envelope. "You be careful with this."

Sometimes grown-ups amaze me. They tell you to act your age and be responsible. Then they treat you like a little baby.

"Come on, Mom," I said. "I won't lose the tickets. I won't get lost. I won't take candy from strangers. I won't chew with my mouth open. I won't—"

Mom held up her hand. "That's enough," she said.

Jason grabbed my arm. "Where did our bags go?"

"Out to the plane," I said.

"Everything's fine," Mom said. "The men will load them on the plane. You'll get them in San Francisco."

Jason shook his head. "Somebody could steal them."

"Nobody would steal your junk," I said.

"What if we get to San Francisco and our bags aren't there?" he asked.

"They'll be there," Mom said. "Let's go to Gate Three." She started walking.

Jason squeezed my arm tighter. "What if our bags aren't there? What if they get lost? Or somebody steals them?"

"Quit worrying," I said. "And quit yelling."

"I want an answer," he said. "And I'm not moving until I get one."

So I gave him an answer. "If our bags aren't there, then the airline people have to buy us all new clothes. And they give us a hundred dollars to buy anything we want." That's not true, of course. But it made him happy.

"I hope my bag's not there," he whispered. "I'll use the money to buy a dog."

Mom was waiting for us up ahead. "This is interesting," she said. "This is where they check for metal. My purse goes on this moving belt." She set her purse down. The belt took it into a big gray machine. "They have a special TV that lets them see what's inside."

"Wow," Jason said.

"Then we go through this doorway over here," I said. "If we had a gun, the buzzer would go off."

Jason looked a little scared. I didn't want him

7

to make a fuss. So I grabbed his arm and took him through the doorway.

"One at a time," the guard said. But Jason and I were already walking through together.

*Bzzzz* went the buzzer.

Jason and I jumped. "I don't have a gun!" Jason yelled.

The guard stepped in front of us. "Go back and try it again," he said. "One at a time."

Jason and I went back. I walked through the doorway again. Nothing happened.

"Okay, little boy," the guard said.

"I'm not a little boy," Jason said. "And I don't have a gun." He walked through.

*Bzzzz* went the buzzer. Jason jumped back.

"Do you have something in your pockets?" the guard asked.

Jason shook his head.

"Are you sure?" Mom asked.

"One more time," the guard said.

By then everybody was looking at Jason. I moved back. I acted like I didn't know him.

Mom patted Jason's pockets. Then she pushed him ahead of her through the doorway.

The buzzer went off again.

The guard picked up a black box. It looked like a radio with lights. "Step over this way, son," he said.

Jason grabbed Mom's hand. "What's that thing?"

"Relax," Mom said. "He's just going to check you for metal."

"I don't have a gun," Jason said again. He looked at me. "Matt, tell him I don't have a gun."

So everybody looked at me and laughed. I hate that.

The guard moved the box over Jason's arms. And chest. And waist. It started to buzz.

"I don't understand this," Mom said. "There's nothing in his pockets."

"He's got something in there," the guard said.

"I guess it's a mistake," Jason said.

The guard shook his head. "No mistake, son."

"Jason," Mom said, "do you have something you're not telling us about?"

Jason looked at the floor.

Just then I figured out what it had to be. "Quit being a dope, Jason," I said. "Pull it out."

"What is it?" Mom asked.

"He's got the dog chain in his underpants," I said.

Jason stuck out his tongue at me. Then he reached into his pants and pulled out the chain.

Everybody laughed. Everybody but Mom and me.

"You know better than this," Mom said. She stuffed the chain into her purse.

"Let's get out of here," I said.

The guard waved us away. And people kept laughing.

"Do you have the tickets?" Mom asked when we got to Gate Three.

She was treating me like a baby again. She'd given me the tickets five minutes ago. And she was sure I'd lost them already.

The envelope was right in my hand. Where else would it be? But I put it behind my back. Then I said, "I thought you had the tickets."

"Oh, no." Mom got a funny look on her face. She started digging in her purse.

"I'm kidding," I said. I waved the envelope in front of her.

She gave me a dirty look. "That's not funny, Matt."

"I'm not two years old," I said.

Mom smiled. "Then don't act like a two-year-old."

It was time for us to get on the plane. Mom hugged us both about six times. "Come on, Mom," I said. "We'll be back in two days."

We gave the man our tickets and went down the ramp. Jason looked back and waved. "Do you think Mom will miss us?" he asked me.

"Think about it," I said. "For two whole days

she won't have to answer any dumb questions. She won't have to clean up any messes. She won't have to tell anybody to turn down the TV. She won't even have to cook. You get the picture?"

"Yeah," Jason said with a smile. "She'll miss us." And he wasn't kidding either.

The funny thing is, he was probably right.

# CHAPTER TWO

We stepped into the plane. "Wow," Jason said. "This is big."

A woman in a blue uniform checked our tickets. "Hi," she said. "I'm Marie."

"I'm Jason. I'm going to San Francisco."

"You have seats Nine E and Nine F," Marie said. "That's nine rows back. Can you count to nine?"

"I can count to a thousand," Jason said. "One, two, three, four—"

Marie moved him down the aisle. "I believe you."

"Excuse me," I said to her. "My little brother likes to play card games. But we forgot our cards. Mom said you might have some."

"Sure, honey." She took a deck of cards out of a cabinet. She handed them to Jason.

"Thank you," Jason said.

"And my little brother has an upset stomach."

"I do *not*," Jason said.

I gave him a push. "Do you think we could get some 7-up for him?"

"Just as soon as we're in the air," she said.

Jason and I went down the aisle. "I don't have an upset stomach," he said.

"I know that," I told him. "But if you say you do, you'll get 7-up right away."

Jason smiled. "Really? How do you know?"

"They did it for a guy last time," I said. "And I saw them bring a woman some cards."

"This is the ninth row," Jason said.

I let him have the seat next to the window. "Buckle your seat belt," I told him.

Jason pulled out the belt. "Why do we need this?"

"It's the rule," I said. "Just like Mom in the car. Buckle up before we move."

"But that's because somebody might run into us. Who's going to run into us up in the sky?"

"It's just a rule," I said.

Jason buckled his belt, then looked around. "Matt," he said, "what if somebody decided not to go on a trip? Could they get their money back?"

I pretended not to hear. I've learned that much from grown-ups. "Look out the window," I said. "Can you see Mom?"

He looked for a minute. "I don't think so."

I leaned over so that I could see out. The people in the building looked about an inch high. "I see her," I said. "She's standing next to the guy in the T-shirt that says 'I Love Tucson.'"

Jason pushed his face up to the window. "Where? How can you see that far?"

It's no fun to tease him. He's too easy. "It was a joke," I said.

"You're the joke," he said. (He heard that line

from me.) Then he said, "Could we get off the plane if we wanted to? I don't want to. But I was just wondering."

"Jason," I said, "do you know how these trays work?" I showed him the trays that folded out of the seat backs in front of us.

He folded and unfolded his tray about ten times. Then he dug into the pouch beneath the tray. He pulled out a magazine and a white paper bag. "What's the bag for?"

"That's what people use if they get sick," I told him.

He looked at the bag and shook his head. "Come on. What's it for?"

"I told you. It's an airsick bag."

He kept shaking his head. "No way."

Just then the airplane motors started. Our seats shook with the noise. Jason grabbed my arm. A man's voice came over the loudspeaker. He told us about emergency exits. Marie stood in the aisle and pointed to them.

Jason wiggled in his seat and dug his fingers

into my arm. "What's emergency?" he asked.

"That's if something bad happens." Jason's mouth dropped open. "Don't worry," I said. "Everything's going to be fine."

The man told about seat belts and oxygen masks. Marie held a mask over her nose. Jason kept wiggling.

Then the man talked about landing in water. He said we could use our seats for life preservers.

That was too much for Jason. He sat up and yelled, "I want to get off!"

Everybody around us laughed.

"Everything's fine," I said.

"I want to get off!" he yelled even louder.

"You can't," I said. "The doors are shut."

Jason's mouth flew open. "You mean we're trapped?" He looked around and started to scream. He didn't scream words, just "Aaaaaaaaaaa."

"Stop it," I said. Everybody in the plane looked at us. I wanted to crawl under the seat.

"Aaaaaaaaaaa," he screamed.

An old man looked back and said, "You're okay, sonny."

A woman behind us asked, "Is he all right?"

"Cut it out," I said.

Jason kept screaming, "Aaaaaaaaaaa."

Marie leaned over me and stuck a piece of candy on Jason's tongue. Jason's mouth snapped shut, and she put a finger on his lips. "Just suck on the candy," she said in a quiet voice. "It's okay to be scared. Lots of people are scared. But it's not okay to yell. If you yell you make other people scared too."

Jason stared at her.

"He's never been on a plane before," I said.

"Everybody's scared the first time," Marie said. "Then they find out how much fun it is. And they're never scared again."

"She's right," I said.

"Now," Marie said, "I want you to put your finger where my finger is."

Jason put a finger across his lips.

She took her finger away. "Here's what we're going to do. First we'll back up." She moved her hand like the airplane, backing up. "Then we'll go out to the runway. Nice and slow."

"It's not scary at all," I said.

"Then we'll crank up the motors. Nice and loud." Marie's hand bounced up and down. "You'll like that. Then we'll go down the runway. Faster and faster. Then we go right up into the air." Her hand went sailing toward the roof.

"Can I take my finger down?" Jason asked. He had to talk out of the side of his mouth.

"In just a second," Marie said. "There's just one more thing. We'll fly for about ten minutes. Then the pilot will turn off the seat belt sign. And I'll bring you a 7-up and a surprise. How's that?"

Jason took away his finger. "What kind of surprise?"

"You'll have to wait and see," Marie said. She went down the aisle.

Jason pushed his nose up against the window. "We're going backward," he said.

"I'll bet it's a neat surprise," I said.

We got to the runway. The engines roared.

"Nice and loud," Jason said. He kept his nose against the window. But he reached over and grabbed my arm.

"It's just the way she said," I told him.

"Matt?" he said. "Matt?"

"Don't scream," I said.

"I won't," he whispered. "But I wish we had parachutes."

We went zipping down the runway. Jason's mouth dropped open. But no sound came out.

Then we were in the air. "We're flying," he said. "We're flying. And I get a surprise."

I leaned back in my seat.

Jason still had his nose against the window. "The ground is way down there," he said. "Way, way down."

"You'll get a surprise in just a minute," I told him. "And a 7-up."

The seat belt light went off. Right away Marie brought Jason silver wings to pin on his shirt. "It's what the pilots wear," she said.

"I wasn't so scared," Jason told her.

"Do you want wings too?" Marie asked me.

That was a tough one. "I'm not a little kid."

"I know," she said. "But I thought you might know somebody who'd like them."

"Good idea." I took the wings and put them in my pocket.

Then we got 7-up. "I brought two," she said to me. "I thought you might have an upset stomach too." She gave us each a bag of peanuts. "Just in case you need a little food."

Jason drank his 7-up and looked out the window. Pretty soon he said, "I have to go potty."

I went along and showed him the tiny bathroom.

He put one foot inside and looked around. "I don't have to go anymore."

"There's nothing to be scared of," I said.

"What do all those signs say?" he asked.

"Just use the potty. You don't have to read the signs."

"I want to know what they say."

So I read him all the signs. I didn't know what some of the signs said. They were in other languages. But I made up things. Like "Don't throw papers on the floor."

Jason stayed in the bathroom a long time. I tapped on the door. "Come on."

He looked out. "The sink's full of water. I can't get it out."

I reached in and pushed down on the handle. The water went out with a big slurp. "Let's go."

"Just a minute." He closed the door again. I could hear the water running, then a big slurp. Then the water. Then another slurp. He didn't quit until I banged on the door.

Marie brought us lunch on trays. It was meat loaf and sliced carrots. "Why is everything wrapped up?" Jason asked her. Everything on the tray was wrapped in plastic. The salad.

The crackers. The cheese. Even the silver.

"It keeps everything clean," Marie said. "And it's like opening birthday presents."

Jason had fun unwrapping everything. But he didn't eat much. "These aren't very good birthday presents," he said.

But we got Cokes for lunch. He liked that. And he had fun opening the little packages of salt and pepper. He poured them on his carrots. Which he wasn't going to eat anyway.

"A 7-up and a Coke and peanuts," Jason said. "I like flying."

"Just do things right in San Francisco," I told him. "Maybe we can do this again."

We couldn't see anything out the window. Just clouds. "How does the pilot know where we are?" Jason asked.

"He uses radar," I said. "He doesn't have to see at all."

"What if the radar didn't work?"

"It always does," I said. "It's a special kind."

"I still wish I had a parachute."

# CHAPTER THREE

"**W**e'll be landing in about three minutes," the pilot said over the loudspeaker.

Jason looked out the window. The clouds were gone. "I don't see the airport."

"We have to be good this weekend," I said. "We want Dad to be happy we came. So we have to be extra nice to Ann and Cathy."

"You've already told me that about a hundred times."

"We need a signal," I said. "To remind us. In case one of us forgets to be good."

"I won't forget," Jason said.

"Just in case. It'll be our secret signal. If one of us forgets, the other can say 'Jelly beans.'"

Jason laughed. "Jelly beans?"

"I might forget, see? I might eat with my fingers. Or pick my nose. And you can say 'Jelly beans.' And I'll quit."

Jason looked out the window again. "You know what's underneath us?"

"The ground," I said.

"No. Water. There's nothing but water down there." He looked over at me. "And I can't swim."

I leaned across him and looked out. I could see hills and houses far away. But there was water right below us. And getting closer every second.

"No problem," I told him. I tried not to sound worried. But I could see the little waves on the water now.

"See how close we are?" he said. "And I can't swim."

By then the water was just below our wings. "I'll take care of you," I said.

He grabbed my arm. "We're going into

the ocean!" Then he let out his yell: "Aaaaaaaaaaa!"

The wheels of the plane smacked down hard. We were on the ground. Not the water.

I leaned back in my seat. "See?" I said. "I told you there was no problem."

Jason looked at me. "Come on, Matt. You were scared too."

"I was *not*," I said. "I knew we'd be fine."

"Me too," Jason said. "I was just playing."

We got out of our seats. Jason grabbed my arm. "What if Dad's not here?"

"He'll be here," I said. "He knows what flight we're on."

"But what if his car didn't work?"

"Quit worrying."

"But what'll we do if he's not here?" Jason said. "I want an answer."

So I gave him one. "If he's not here, we'll sit down and wait for him." Jason still looked worried. So I added, "And I'll buy you a candy bar to eat while we wait."

Jason smiled. "What kind of candy bar?"

"Any kind you want."

He kept smiling. "I hope Dad's late."

We came up the ramp and saw Dad. "Hi, Daddy," Jason yelled. He ran past people and hugged Dad. I hung back a little. I'm too old for hugging. Dad grabbed my shoulder. "It's good to see you," he said.

Jason jumped up and down. "We got 7-up and Coke and peanuts and yukky meat loaf. And the plane almost went into the water. Did you bring the dog?"

Dad picked up Jason and hugged him again. "I've missed you guys," he said. He set Jason down and looked at me. "Matt, I'd pick you up too. But I'm not strong enough."

"Are Ann and Cathy here?" I asked.

"They couldn't make it," Dad said. "They'll see you at the house. Ann can't wait to meet you boys."

I was glad they weren't there. I wanted to see

Dad first. But I said, "We want to meet her too."

"And the dog," Jason said.

It was a long walk to the baggage area. Every minute or two Dad would ask me a question. Like "How was your trip?" and "How's school going?"

"Fine," I answered. He wasn't listening anyway.

"I hope our bags aren't there," Jason whispered to me. "I want the money."

"What money?" I asked.

"The hundred dollars. So I can buy a dog."

I'd forgotten I'd told him that.

But a minute later he grabbed my arm. "I don't want the money."

"Why not?"

"I forgot about Willie," Jason said. "He's in my bag." Willie is Jason's toy dog. Jason sleeps with him every night.

The baggage area was crowded. Dad lifted Jason so he could see. The bags came out of the chute and slid onto the moving belt. "I don't see mine," Jason said.

"It'll be here soon," Dad told him.

"What if it got put on the wrong plane?" Jason said. "Or maybe somebody took it. Willie will be scared." He pushed through the people and got next to the belt. Each time a bag came out of the chute, he said, "Nope. Nope."

"Don't worry," Dad said.

But Jason wasn't listening. He had his eyes on the chute. And he kept saying, "Nope. Nope. Nope."

Then his blue bag came out of the chute. He screamed loud enough for the whole airport to hear: "That's mine!"

"I'll get it," Dad said.

But Jason was gone.

He jumped up onto the belt, stepped over some golf clubs, and grabbed that blue bag. He hauled it off the belt. "It got here. All the way from Tucson. It got here."

Of course he had to open the bag. He had to be sure Willie was all right. He hugged Willie, then put him back in the bag. "Willie was a little scared," Jason said. "But he's okay now."

Dad drove around and showed us the city. I got my camera out of my bag. I wanted to take lots of pictures. I was going to show them to my class back in Tucson.

We went across the Golden Gate Bridge. We parked and walked to a lookout spot. We could see the city and the bridge. And sailboats and islands. I took six pictures.

Dad pointed out Alcatraz, an island where there was an old prison. Then he told us the names of some of the buildings across the way. It was hard to tell which ones he meant.

"This is really great," I said.

Jason whispered in my ear, "When can we go see his dog?"

"Pretty soon," I said.

"I hope so," Jason said. "I'm tired of looking at stuff."

"Act interested," I said. "We don't want to hurt Dad's feelings."

We went back across the bridge and drove through Golden Gate Park. Dad told us things about San Francisco. I kept looking back at Jason. He wasn't even looking at the stuff Dad showed us. He had his head against the window. And pretty soon he closed his eyes.

I reached back and grabbed his knee. "Jelly beans," I whispered.

We ended up at the beach. Dad stopped the car by a stone wall. We looked out at the waves. "That's the Pacific Ocean," Dad said. "Nothing but water for thousands of miles."

"Wow," Jason said. "Let's go."

We went down cement steps to the beach. Jason and I took off our shoes and socks. The sand was cold on my feet. But I liked the way it squeezed between my toes.

"Can we go wading?" I asked.

"The water's pretty cold," Dad said.

"We can take it," I said.

Dad waved us away. "Go ahead."

We ran for the water. Jason slowed down when we got close. "Come on," I said. "We'll just get our toes wet."

He grabbed my hand. "Are there any sharks in here?"

We moved close to the water. Then we stopped and watched the wave come up the sand and over our feet.

Dad was wrong. The water wasn't pretty cold. It was freezing. It was like sticking your toes into snow. Only colder.

"Yikes," Jason said, running out of the water. "I can't stand it." But he ran back into the next wave. And the next. And the next. "Yikes," he kept yelling.

Jason started to make a sand castle. He used his hands to scoop the sand into a big pile. Then he patted the sand into walls. "I wish I had a shovel," he said.

I went to a trash can and found him a big paper cup. Jason packed the cup full of sand.

Then he used the packed sand for towers.

Dad kept looking at his watch. "We'd better go," he said.

"Just a few more minutes," Jason begged. "Please. Just a few more minutes. I'm not quite done."

Finally Dad said we had to go. Jason begged to stay. But Dad said no.

"Come on, Jason," I said. I was afraid he was going to cry.

Jason stood up and looked at his castle. "It's not done," he said.

"Maybe you can come back and finish it," I told him.

"Can I, Dad?" Jason asked. "Can I come back and finish it?"

"Not this time," Dad told him. "We've got a lot of great things to do this weekend."

Jason was mad. I could tell by his face. "Jelly beans," I whispered.

Jason lifted up his bare foot and smacked it down on one of his towers.

"Don't do that," I said.

Jason jumped up and down on the castle. Soon there was nothing left but a pile of sand.

I ran over to Dad. "He's just having fun," I said. I couldn't tell if Dad believed me.

We walked toward the car. "I have something great to show you, Jason," Dad said. "Have you ever heard of Lombard Street?"

Jason didn't answer. So I said, "What is it?"

"It's the crookedest street in the world. We'll go down it on our way home."

"That'll be neat," I said. "I want to get a picture."

"Who cares about the crookedest street in the world?" Jason whispered to me.

"Don't be a brat," I told him. "We want Dad to have a good time."

"Go jump in the ocean," Jason said.

# CHAPTER FOUR

Dad's house was different from Tucson houses. It didn't have a front yard. And it was built right up against other houses.

Jason jumped out of the car. "Where's the dog?"

"He's out in back," Dad said.

"Can I see him?"

"Sure," Dad said. "But first I want you to meet Ann and Cathy."

"I'd rather see the dog," Jason whispered to me.

I gave him a shove.

We went up the front steps and into the house. Ann and Cathy were waiting for us. "I'm so glad to meet you boys," Ann said. She shook our hands, but she didn't try to hug us. I liked that.

Cathy was littler than I expected. She hid behind her mother and peeked at us. "Hi, Cathy," I said.

For just a second her tongue poked out. Then she hid her face.

"Say hi to Jason and Matt," Dad told her.

"No," Cathy said.

I was glad she was being rotten. I didn't want Dad's new family to be too perfect.

"She's a little shy," Ann told us.

"Am not," Cathy said.

"How was your flight, Matt?" Ann asked me.

"Fine," I said. But I was watching Jason. I wanted him to get off to a good start.

"Cathy, why don't you show Jason your toys?" Dad said.

She had some neat toys on the table. Not just dolls and teddy bears. She had dinosaurs and

trucks and an airplane. Right away Jason picked up a tow truck.

"That's mine," Cathy said. She grabbed it out of his hands.

Jason started to grab it back. "Jelly beans," I whispered.

Ann smiled at me. "Jelly beans?"

Jason gave me a dirty look. But he let her have the truck.

"We know it's your toy," Dad told Cathy in a quiet voice. "But Jason would like to see it."

Cathy started to cry. "But I want to play with it."

"That's okay," Jason said. "I'll play with this one." He picked up a tractor.

"That's mine," Cathy said, reaching for it. "Give it to me."

For a second I thought Jason might give it to her. Right in the face.

But he handed her the tractor and grabbed an airplane. And, of course, Cathy wanted that.

Jason turned the whole thing into a game. He picked up a bus. Then a dinosaur. Then a rag doll. And Cathy grabbed them from him. Pretty soon she couldn't hold all the toys.

And when she dropped one, Jason would pick it up. And she'd say, "I want that. It's mine."

"Why don't you pick out one for Jason to play with?" Ann said.

Cathy stuck out her lip and shook her head.

"Jason," Dad said, "let's go see Ben."

Jason and I went to the backyard with Dad. Cathy wanted to come with us. Probably to keep us from touching her dog. But Ann said no.

"Give Cathy a little time," Dad told us. "She's only four years old."

"No problem, Dad," Jason said. "She's just a brat."

I gave Jason a dirty look and whispered, "Jelly beans."

"Well, she is," Jason said.

Dad smiled. "Sometimes."

"I used to be a brat," Jason said.

I gave him a push. "You're still a brat. Sometimes." I was teasing him. But what I said was the truth.

We walked down the back steps. Dad called Ben. Ben crawled out of the doghouse. He was just a regular black dog. A sleepy regular black dog. He yawned and walked over to us.

Jason started petting him. "He's neat." Ben wagged his tail—slowly.

"Does he do any tricks?" I asked Dad.

"He only has one trick," Dad said. "I bring him his dinner and say, 'Eat.' And he eats. That's about it."

"That's what I thought."

Ben flopped on the ground. Jason kept petting him. "He's really neat, Dad."

I couldn't figure out why Jason was so happy. I didn't hate the dog or anything. But he was about as exciting as a dish of oatmeal. With no sugar or raisins.

"Can I sleep with him tonight?" Jason asked.

"I'm afraid not," Dad said. "Ben doesn't come in the house."

"That's okay," Jason said. "I can sleep with him out here."

We went to Chinatown for dinner. We walked along and looked in the store windows. We saw T-shirts and Chinese clothes. And lamps. And more T-shirts. I liked the food stores best. Ann showed me funny stuff for sale. Like dried octopus.

Jason held Dad's hand. Cathy took Dad's other hand.

"Look at this," Jason said. He pulled Dad toward the window.

"Look at *this*," Cathy said. She pulled Dad the other way.

"Jelly beans," I whispered to Jason. "Jelly beans."

We went into a restaurant. We got a table by the window. "What would you like?" Dad asked me. He showed me the menu. It was all in Chinese.

I laughed. Then I pointed at some letters. "I want that. And that."

"Okay," Dad said. "Matt wants bird's nest soup and fried octopus. What about the rest of you?"

"Wait a minute," I said. And Dad laughed.

Dad ordered for all of us. Then he and Ann showed us how to use chopsticks.

Jason wasn't too good with them. "What if I can't use them?" he asked. "How can I eat?"

Dad and Ann answered at the same time. Dad said, "They can bring you a fork." Ann said, "You can always use your fingers."

Jason smiled at Ann. He liked her answer better.

"I can sing 'The A-B-C Song,'" Cathy said. "A-B-C-D-E-F-G—"

"Let's not sing," Ann said.

But Cathy sang the whole thing. Two times.

Ann took a peanut butter sandwich out of her purse. "Cathy's a little young for Chinese food," she said.

"But I eat my sandwich with chopsticks," Cathy said. She speared her sandwich with a chopstick. Then she ate it like an ice-cream bar.

Some of the food was pretty good. Some was pretty bad. I pretended to like everything, of course. "This is great," I kept saying. I hoped Jason would get the idea. But he didn't.

"This brown stuff is yucky," he said.

I kicked him. "It's kind of good too," he said. "Kind of yucky and good." Mostly he ate rice. Then he ate the rest of Cathy's peanut butter sandwich.

After the meal the waiter brought us fortune cookies.

"What are these?" Jason asked.

"They're fortune cookies," Ann said. "Take one."

Jason took one. He popped it into his mouth and started to chew.

Dad and I broke out laughing. Jason looked at us. He didn't know what was funny. And he kept chewing.

"Hold it," I said. "Don't swallow anything." I grabbed a fortune cookie. I broke it open and showed him the paper inside.

Jason's face turned red. He reached into his mouth and took out a soggy paper. "Why didn't you tell me?" he said.

"What did it taste like?" Cathy asked him.

Jason smiled. "Like candy. Only better."

We read our fortunes. Then I saw Cathy sneak her paper into her mouth.

Back at the house Dad had a video for us. It was about whales. Jason watched it for about two minutes. Then he went to sleep. I saw most of it, I think. But I dozed off once or twice.

Finally Dad got out sleeping bags for Jason

and me. He put them on the living room floor. We brushed our teeth and put on our pajamas. Then Jason wanted to say good night to Ben. "I want Ben to meet Willie."

"Let's make it quick," Dad said.

I was too tired to go with them. I slid into my bag and went right to sleep.

Jason woke me up by poking me in the back. "Matt," he said. "Matt. Are you asleep?"

"Yes."

"If you're asleep, how come you're talking?"

"I must be dreaming," I said.

"I can't sleep, Matt. The floor's too hard. And I'm not tired."

"No wonder you're not tired," I said. "You slept clear through the video."

"Matt, did you really like that Chinese food?"

"Some of it was okay."

"You acted like it was great."

"You gotta tell people what they want to hear," I said.

Jason was quiet for a minute. Then he said, "What does an earthquake sound like?"

"I don't know."

"I think I just heard one."

"That was the heater coming on."

"What if there was an earthquake? What would we do?"

"Go to sleep," I told him.

"Listen," he said after a minute. "I think I hear something."

"It's not an earthquake," I said.

"Somebody's walking around. It might be a burglar."

"It's not a burglar."

"Willie's kind of scared," Jason said. "Maybe I ought to get Ben in here. He could guard us."

"They don't let Ben in the house."

"We could put him out before they get up. Then Willie wouldn't be scared."

I was too tired to argue. We sneaked Ben into the house. Jason put his arm around Ben and

went to sleep. I almost went to sleep too. But
Ben came over and licked my ear. I thought
about putting him outside again. But it was eas-
ier to snuggle down in my sleeping bag. And
cover up my ear.

# CHAPTER FIVE

Dad woke us early the next morning. "Let's go, boys," he called out. Then he saw Ben lying on Jason's sleeping bag. "How'd he get in?"

I didn't say anything. I figured Dad already knew the answer to that one.

Dad came over and grabbed Ben's collar. "Didn't I explain that Ben doesn't come in the house?" He was trying not to yell at us. But he was having trouble.

Jason smiled at Dad. "Willie was scared. We needed Ben to guard us."

Dad didn't smile back. "He's not an inside dog. I told you that." He turned and led Ben away.

"He liked sleeping with us," Jason said. "And he didn't hurt anything."

Dad stopped and looked back at us. "Take a look in the corner. He had an accident right there." He and Ben went out the door.

Jason looked over at the corner. "Did Ben do that?"

"It sure wasn't me," I said. So now we knew why Ben wasn't an inside dog. Now that it was too late.

"I wonder why Dad calls it an accident," Jason said.

"Don't ask him that right now," I said.

Dad came back with some paper towels and a bowl of soapy water.

"Do you want us to clean it up?" I asked. I hoped he'd say no.

"Go ahead and get dressed," Dad said quietly. "I'll take care of it." I could tell that he was holding himself back. In a way I wished he'd let go and yell at us. We had it coming. But I was glad he didn't.

Jason and I got dressed in the bathroom. I helped him comb his hair. We came out and saw Ann. She was using a machine to scrub the carpet.

"Good morning," I said.

She smiled at us. Sort of. And she kept scrubbing.

"I'm sorry," I said.

She waved me away and smiled again. Sort of.

We had toaster waffles for breakfast. Jason thought they were great. He'd seen them on TV. But he'd never had one before.

"Ann was going to fix something else," Dad said. "But she wanted to clean the carpet right away. And we've got a big day ahead of us."

"These are great," I said.

The first thing we did was ride the cable car. I got some good pictures.

Jason liked the cable car. Until Dad explained how it worked. Dad said the car was hooked to an underground cable.

We were just starting down a steep hill. "What if it slips off the cable?" Jason asked.

"It can't," I told him. "It's impossible."

But Jason had to check with Dad. "Dad, has a cable car ever gotten loose and crashed?"

"I don't think so," Dad said. "Maybe once in fifty years."

That was once too often. Jason held on to the seat with both hands and screamed "Aaaaaaaaaaa." All the way to the bottom of the hill.

After riding the cable car, we took Dad's car to the aquarium. Inside the front door was the reptile room. You could look over a railing and see a bunch of alligators down below. They all looked asleep.

"Let's go," Jason said. "Right now."

"Don't worry," I told him. "They can't climb up here."

"What if somebody left a ladder in there?"

"Alligators can't climb ladders," I said.

I hurried him past the snakes in glass cages. He didn't need to see any rattlesnakes.

We looked through the windows at the fish. "What if the glass breaks?" he asked. But he didn't sound too worried.

It was almost feeding time for the penguins. Dad left us for a few minutes. He wanted to check on the planetarium show.

Jason and I could see fine at first. I got my camera all ready. Then some grown-ups crowded in front of us.

"Excuse me," I said. "We can't see."

But it was the same old story. We were just kids. So they didn't even look down at us.

"Let's go," Jason said. "I can't see anything."

"Excuse me," I said, louder than before. "Can we get in front of you?"

"It's no use," Jason said. "They won't listen to you."

"We'll make them listen," I said.

I whispered my plan to him. He started to giggle.

I moved up close to the grown-ups and yelled out, "Are you sure you're going to throw up? I told you not to eat three hot dogs."

The people in front of us heard *that*. Right away they started to move.

Then Jason made growling noises. And the people really moved.

So we got a good look at the penguins. And I got three great pictures.

We decided not to tell Dad what we'd done. Grown-ups don't always understand those things.

We ate hamburgers in the cafeteria. We watched a show at the planetarium. Then we drove across town to the zoo.

On the way Jason whispered to me, "Do we have to go to the zoo?"

Most days he would have loved the zoo. But he was tired by then.

"Dad's trying to give us a good time," I said. "We don't want to hurt his feelings."

"But I'm tired," Jason said.

I didn't want to mess up Dad's plans. But I didn't want Jason to get tired and fussy. So I stretched out my arms and yawned. "I'm kind of tired."

Dad looked over at me and laughed. "You're not too tired for the zoo, are you?"

"I guess not," I said.

"You guess not?" Dad looked back at Jason. "What are we going to do with this guy, Jason? A big guy like him, and he's too tired to go see the lions and tigers. You're not tired, are you?"

"Not me," Jason said. "I feel fine." And he stuck out his tongue when I gave him a dirty look.

So we went to the zoo. And Jason was tired and grouchy.

Dad seemed tired too.

I wondered if he was tired of us.

We got back to Dad's place late in the afternoon. Ann was already cooking dinner. Cathy was happy to see us. Until she found out we'd been to the zoo. Then she cried.

"I want to go to the zoo," she said.

"Why don't you get your cards?" Ann told her.

Cathy picked up her cards. "You want to play Slap Jack?" she asked Jason.

"I want to see Ben," Jason said. He headed for the backyard.

I didn't want Cathy crying again. So I said, "I'll play with you."

If you've never heard of Slap Jack, you're lucky. It's the easiest card game in the world. Each player gets half the cards. You take turns flipping over a card and putting it on a pile. If you flip over a jack, you both try to slap it. The one who slaps it first gets all the cards in the pile. You get the idea? And it's just as dumb as it sounds. Maybe dumber.

Right away I made a bad mistake. I slapped a jack. Cathy said it wasn't fair. She said I was mean.

So the dumb game got even dumber. I sat there and flipped cards with her. She won five games. And I didn't slap one jack.

She smiled at me. "I'm a good player."

"You're the greatest," I said.


Jason came back inside. Cathy wanted to play cards with him. "Matt's too easy," she said.

I took Jason aside and whispered, "Let her win."

Jason shook his head. "No way."

"Don't start trouble," I told him. But I knew what was coming.

That game didn't last very long. About three jacks long, I think. By then Cathy was crying. "You cheat!" she yelled.

Jason was ready to stop playing Slap Jack and start playing Slap Cathy.

I grabbed him and took him into the hall. "I told you to let her win."

"She's nothing but a brat," Jason said.

"I know," I said. "But we've got to get along with her. If we don't, Dad won't want us here."

Dad came out of the kitchen. "Jason," he said, "let's take Ben for a walk." That made everybody happy.

Everybody but me. I had to play Slap Jack again.

Jason and I washed our hands before dinner. "Be sure and say everything's great," I told him.

"I know that," he said.

"Just do it," I said. "Tell 'em what they want to hear."

Jason did say everything was great. It was easy that time. Ann had made all his favorites. Chicken. Mashed potatoes. Peas. And chocolate pudding.

After dinner Ann brought out a box of Lego blocks. "We need your help, Jason," she said.

"Could you show Cathy how to make some things?"

Cathy and Jason made houses. And cars. And a funny-looking dog.

Dad set up the chessboard. I hadn't played chess since Dad moved to San Francisco. But I still remembered how.

We played a long game. Dad made lots of mistakes. And I finally won. "Good job," he said.

I was happy for a second. Then I started thinking. Dad was a good chess player. Why did he make so many mistakes?

I looked over at him. "You let me win, didn't you?"

He just smiled.

"You did, didn't you?"

"You're just learning the game," he said.

I leaned close to him and whispered, "I'm not like Cathy playing Slap Jack. I won't cry if I lose."

Dad smiled. "I know. I was just giving you practice."

"Well, don't," I said. "I want you to try as hard as you can."

"All right," Dad said.

We had three very short games. He smashed me in no time at all.

I didn't cry. But I didn't have much fun either. I decided I should have kept my mouth shut.

# CHAPTER SIX

I didn't get much sleep that night. At midnight Jason thought we were having an earthquake. (We weren't.)

Around one o'clock he thought he heard a burglar. (He didn't.)

Then he tiptoed outside. He had to make sure the burglar hadn't stolen Ben. (He hadn't.)

He brought Ben inside for a minute. He thought Ben was cold. (Maybe he was.)

Later Jason tried to sneak Ben into his sleeping bag. He hoped I wouldn't hear. (I did. And so did Dad. And out went Ben.)

Jason poked me in the back. "What do

you think Mom's doing right now?" he whispered.

"Sleeping," I said. "If she's lucky."

"Do you like San Francisco?" he asked.

"Sure. Don't you?"

"It's okay," Jason said. "But Willie wants to be back in his own bed."

Dad got us up early again. "I have a great surprise for you today," he said. "You get three guesses."

I was too sleepy to guess. "What is it?"

"You have to guess," Dad said. "It's a special treat."

"Can I go to the bathroom first?" Jason asked.

I couldn't think of anything to guess. We'd already done all the special things yesterday. Then I saw the picnic basket in Dad's hand. "A picnic?"

"Better than that," Dad said. "Jason, what's your guess?"

"I have to go to the bathroom," Jason said. "Now." He took off running.

"You remember the whale video?" Dad said to me. "This time it won't be on TV."

"What do you mean?" I said.

"We're taking a boat out into the ocean," Dad said. "If we're lucky, we'll see whales."

"You mean it?" I asked. "We're going right out there with the whales?"

"We can't be sure about seeing whales," Dad said. "I hope we do. But it'll be a great trip anyway. We'll go out to a bunch of islands. We'll see lots of seals and birds."

Jason came back in a minute. "We're taking a boat ride," I told him. "We might see whales. If we're lucky. And I'm going to get a picture."

"How big are the whales?" Jason asked.

"Whales only come in two sizes," Dad said. "Big and bigger."

Jason looked at me. "Are they big enough to eat a boat?"

"That's just in the stupid cartoons," I told

him. "The whales won't eat our boat." I went off to the bathroom.

I heard Jason asking, "Could they? Could they eat a boat if they wanted to?"

"They wouldn't want to," Dad said. "Whales eat little tiny plants that float in the water."

"But what if they wanted to eat a boat?" Jason went on. "Could they do it?"

For breakfast Ann made a special kind of pancakes. They had nuts and blueberries in them. "These are great," I said.

I kicked Jason. "These are great," he said.

They were all right. But not as good as toaster waffles.

After breakfast Jason and I put on our warmest clothes. We didn't have any mittens. So Ann brought me some of hers. They were pink with yellow flowers. I wasn't going to wear those things. I didn't care how cold it was.

But I said, "These are great. But don't you need them?"

"Cathy and I aren't going," she said. "She's a little young. And you boys need some time alone with your dad."

I was glad to hear that. But I didn't say so.

Jason's mittens had the three little kittens on them. But he didn't even look at them. "Dad," he said, "I don't feel good."

"Wait'll you get out on that boat," Dad said. "You'll feel better right away. We're going to sail right under the Golden Gate Bridge."

Jason sniffed. "I think I might be coming down with a cold. Or maybe the flu."

Dad just laughed. "Don't worry, son. The sea air will fix you up right away. You'll feel like a million dollars in no time."


We drove down to Fisherman's Wharf. Jason started asking about whales again.

"Don't worry, Jason," Dad said. "The whales won't eat the boat."

"What if they got too close?" Jason said. "Couldn't they tip the boat over?"

"Everything's going to be fine," Dad said.

"I can't swim," Jason said.

"You'll have on a life vest," Dad said. "Everybody will. But you won't need it. It's perfectly safe."

Jason shook his head. "If it's safe, why does everybody wear life vests?"

"Quit worrying," I said. "This is going to be fun."

"I don't feel good," Jason said.

"Look at all the boats," Dad said. We drove past some piers. I could smell the ocean. And stinky fish.

"I really don't feel good," Jason said.

Dad found a place to park. He opened the trunk. He gave Jason a blanket to carry. He handed me the picnic basket. Then he gathered up coats and bags and blankets. "All right," he said. "Let's do it."

I had to put my camera around my neck. I needed both hands to lift the picnic basket. "What's in here?" I asked.

"I put in lots of goodies," Dad said. "The sea air makes you hungry." He headed across the parking lot. "Follow me." I rushed along behind him.

It was hard carrying the basket. My knees bumped it with each step. And my arms ached. I stopped at the edge of the parking lot. "Let's rest a second," I called out.

"Sure," Dad said. "I can take the basket if you want." Then he looked past me. "Where's Jason?"

I looked toward the parking lot. "He's gotta be right here." I ran back a few steps and looked. "He's gotta be."

But he wasn't.

We couldn't see Jason anywhere.

# CHAPTER SEVEN

"I guess we walked too fast," Dad said. "Wait here with our stuff. I'll run back and get him."

But I knew something was wrong. "Can I go back to the car too?" I asked. "Please."

"All right," Dad said. "But let's hurry." He started to run. The stuff he was carrying bounced up and down with each step.

I grabbed up the picnic basket and followed him.

"Jason!" Dad called. "Jason! We're coming."

"He's probably sitting in the car," I called out. I didn't believe that. But I wanted to say something. Anything.

"The car's locked," Dad said. Then he called, "Jason! Where are you, son?"

We ran until we could see our car. Jason wasn't there.

Dad stopped and called, "Jason!"

We stood and listened. All I could hear was my breathing. And my heart pounding.

Dad called three more times. People on the street turned and looked our way.

"Hey, Jason," I yelled. That was stupid. Dad's voice was twice as loud as mine. But I felt like yelling.

Then Dad grabbed the basket from me. "Let's get rid of this stuff." He ran ahead of me and opened the trunk. He dumped everything in and slammed the trunk lid. "Jason!" he called once more.

"What'll we do?" I asked. "Shall we call the police?"

"We'll look for him first," Dad said. "He can't be far. You go down this street for two blocks. Straight down. If you don't find him, come right back here. Ask people if they've seen him."

"All right," I said.

"Just two blocks," Dad said. "Then come right back. Wait for me here."

I raced down the street. Behind me I could hear Dad calling Jason.

Not many people were on the sidewalk. A woman with a big ring of keys was unlocking a store. "Excuse me," I called. "Have you seen a little boy around here?"

The woman shook her head. "You're the only boy I've seen. Who's missing?"

"My little brother."

"Don't worry," she said. "You'll find him."

I hurried past a kite store. Above the door was an elephant kite and a dragon kite. Jason would have liked those kites.

I passed a wax museum. A man was in the ticket booth. I reached up and tapped on the window. "We're not open yet," he said.

"My brother's lost," I called. "Have you seen a little kid?"

"Sorry." He shook his head. "Don't worry. He'll show up."

That's grown-ups for you. They all said not to worry. Why shouldn't I worry? My little brother was lost.

There was a fish market right on the sidewalk. A man in a white apron was stirring a huge pot. "My brother's lost," I told him. "He's a little guy. Did you see him go by?"

"No," the man said. "He didn't go by here."

"What about on the other side of the street?"

The man took a big wooden spoon out of the pot. "He didn't come this way, son."

"Thanks." I turned and started away.

"You want a doughnut?" he called after me.

"I've got to find my brother," I yelled.

Dad had told me to go down two blocks and then come back. But that would be a waste of time now. So I went up a side street. I wasn't supposed to do that. But I didn't care. I wanted to find Jason.

I ran to the end of the block. I didn't see

Jason. I didn't even see anybody to ask.

I saw a cable car up ahead of me. The bell was ringing. I ran toward it, then stopped. I knew better than that. I wasn't sure what Jason might do. But I knew one thing he wouldn't do. He wouldn't ride a cable car.

I turned and ran back to the parking lot.

I stood on the sidewalk and waited for Dad. I started thinking about Jason. I hadn't had time to think before.

I thought about how scared Jason was of everything. He was scared of boats. He thought a whale would eat him. But he'd also be too scared to do anything else. He wouldn't walk very far. He'd be afraid of getting lost. And he wouldn't ride a cable car. And he wouldn't go anywhere with a stranger.

Where would a scared little guy go?

And then I knew where he had to be. It was the only place he'd go. I should have known from the start.

I spotted Dad far up the street. He was racing along the sidewalk. He disappeared into a store. A few seconds later he came running back out.

I headed toward him. "Dad!" I yelled. I waved my arm over my head. "Dad!"

Dad waved back. Then he ran to meet me. "Where's Jason?" he called out. "Did you find him?"

I couldn't get my breath to yell. I just waved my arms.

Dad ran up to me. Sweat was running down his face. "Where is he?" he asked.

"He's fine," I said. "Look, Dad, don't be mad at him."

"I'm not mad," Dad said in a loud voice. "I'm just worried."

"He was just scared. Really scared."

"About what? The boat?"

"About everything. I guess he thought a whale might eat us. And he can't swim. So he's scared of the water."

Dad nodded. "I knew he was a little scared. But I didn't think it was a big deal. Why didn't he say something?"

It took me a second to answer. I didn't want Dad to get mad. But I was thinking about Jason right then. "You know what, Dad?" I said finally. "He did say something. He said a lot. But we didn't listen."

"You're right, Matt." Dad looked down the street. "But where is he?"

"Come on," I said. "I'll show you."

We walked back to the parking lot. Dad kept looking around. He still hadn't figured things out.

When we got to the car, I got down on my knees. "Look," I whispered. Dad squatted down beside me.

Underneath our car, wrapped up in the blanket, was my scared little brother.

# CHAPTER EIGHT

"Don't be mad at him, Dad," I whispered.

"I'm not mad," Dad said. "I'm just sorry this happened."

Jason was rolled up in the blanket. He wasn't moving at all. I wondered if he was asleep.

Dad got down on his knees. He reached out and patted Jason. "Hey, son, this is no place to take a nap."

The blanket wiggled. But Jason didn't say anything.

"Come on out," Dad said. "The boat ride's off. I hope you don't mind too much."

Jason slid out from under the car. He had sand stuck in his hair. His face was all red. And his cheeks were wet. He wouldn't look at us.

Dad brushed off Jason's hair. "I was worried about you, son. I'm sorry this happened."

Jason kept his eyes on the ground. I tried to think of a joke or something.

Finally Dad said, "You guys want some hot chocolate?"

I didn't. But I wanted to quit standing there. "Sure," I said.

Jason rubbed his eyes. "I don't care."

"We need to go somewhere and talk," Dad said. "We have to plan our day. And I could use some coffee."

"We can get some down this way," I said. "And the guy has doughnuts too."

"Sounds good," Dad said. "What do you think, Jason? Could you use a doughnut?"

"I guess so," Jason said.

We walked down the street to the seafood stand. "I see you found your brother," the man in the white apron said.

"I wasn't lost," Jason said.

"Everything's fine now," I said.

Jason and I took our hot chocolate and doughnuts over to a bench. Two sea gulls came over to us. They tried to peck our doughnuts. Jason held his doughnut behind his back. And he tried to pat the birds with his other hand.

Dad shooed the birds away. Then he sat down between us. "It's my fault," he said. "I was so happy you guys were coming. I wanted every-thing to be great for you."

"It *has* been great, Dad," I said.

He squeezed my arm. "I miss seeing you two. And I wanted everything to be perfect. So I made all kinds of plans. But I forgot to ask you guys what you wanted. And I'm sorry."

"It's our fault too, Dad," I said. "We didn't tell you what we thought."

"It's *your* fault," Jason said to me. "You said we shouldn't hurt Dad's feelings."

"We'll talk about this later, Jason," I said.

But Jason wasn't about to stop. "Matt keeps saying, 'Tell 'em what they want to hear.'"

"Jelly beans," I said.

"And he thinks I'm being bad all the time," Jason went on. "So he says, 'Jelly beans.' That's to tell me to be good. But I'm being as good as I can."

"I think you're doing fine," Dad said.

"Matt doesn't," Jason said. "He thinks I'm bad. And he says you might not want us anymore if I'm bad. 'Cause you have a new family now."

"That's not what—" I began.

Dad surprised me right then. I thought he'd be mad. Or maybe unhappy. But he laughed out loud.

Jason and I looked at each other. We couldn't figure it out.

"We're something," Dad said. "We're all scared we'll do something wrong." He wrapped one arm around Jason and one around me. "I was just like Matt. I wanted everything to be perfect. But I was trying too hard. I needed somebody to say 'Jelly beans' to me."

"Jelly beans," Jason said. He giggled.

"Look, boys," Dad said. "I'll still like you if you do something wrong." Then he laughed again. "What about you? If I do something dumb, is it okay? Will you still like me?"

"Sure," I said.

"I always like you," Jason said.

Dad gave us both a squeeze. "Matt's not all wrong," Dad said. "Sometimes you can't say what you think. You might see a person with an ugly dog. You can't go up and say, 'Your dog is ugly.'"

That made Jason and me laugh out loud.

"But with our friends and family," Dad went on, "it's better to be honest."

"See?" Jason said to me.

A sea gull landed next to Jason's foot. He tossed it a little piece of his doughnut.

"Your bird is ugly," I said. "You're my family. So I can say that."

Jason started to laugh. "Your face is ugly."

"Boys," Dad said, "I want you to do just

what Matt said. Tell me what I want to hear."

"What?" Jason said.

"You mean it?" I asked.

Dad laughed. "I mean it. Tell me what I want to hear. But what I want to hear is the truth. And nothing but the truth. I want to hear how you feel. What you like. What you don't. And I'll do the same with you." He held out his hand to me. "Is it a deal?"

I shook his hand. "It's a deal."

"You bet," Jason said. He slapped Dad's hand the way ballplayers do.

"So let's start over," Dad said. "Today's a free day. No plans at all. And Jason gets to decide what we do."

I turned to Jason. "What do you want to do?"

Jason smiled and chewed on his doughnut. "I don't care."

"That's a big help," I said.

"Think about it for a minute," Dad said. "We can do anything you want."

Jason looked at him. "Anything?"

"Just about," Dad said.

"Then I want to go back to the beach and make a sand castle."

"Sounds great," Dad said. "What else?"

"That's all," Jason said.

Dad started to say something, then stopped. "You're the boss," he said.

"And one other thing," Jason said.

"What's that?"

"I want to feed the rest of my doughnut to the birds."

So he fed his doughnut to the sea gulls. And some crackers too.

We walked back to the car. "Can we get a shovel?" Jason asked.

"I have a great shovel back at the house," Dad said. "We'll go by and pick it up."

"Can we take Ben to the beach?" Jason asked. "He'd like to run around in the sand."

"Sure," Dad said. "Maybe Cathy and Ann will want to go too."

I thought Jason might not want to take Cathy. But he just smiled and said, "I can teach Cathy to make a castle."

So we all went to the beach. Jason and I tried to take Ben for a run in the sand. But Ben liked walking better than running. And he liked lying down better than walking.

Jason and Cathy started making a castle. Ben lay in the sand and watched them.

Dad and I took a long walk up the beach. "I'm sorry you missed the boat ride," he said.

"It's okay."

"We'll do it soon," Dad said. "I mean it. If Jason's not ready, you and I can go."

When we came back, the castle was huge. "See this?" Cathy said. "This is the living room. And here's the kitchen. And here's a bedroom for the king. And one for the queen."

We had a giant lunch. And we didn't eat half the stuff in the basket. We all sat on the blanket. We were too full to move.

"Matt and Jason didn't understand something," Dad said. "They thought my new family was Ann and Cathy."

"They are," Jason said.

"Come here," Dad said. "All of you. Closer. You too, Matt." We scooted in close. Dad wrapped his arms around all four of us.

Jason tried to hug everybody too. "Sardines in a can," he said.

"This is my new family," Dad said. "Ann and Cathy. And Matt. And Jason. I'm glad we can be together."

We sat there with our arms around each other. People on the beach stared at us.

But I didn't care a bit.


Jason and Cathy worked on the castle some more. Dad helped them for a while. Ann and I sat on the blanket. She asked me about the desert. I told her about Tucson. And about my school.

Then Dad and Ann and I threw a Frisbee. Cathy and Jason kept playing in the sand. Pretty soon the castle had bedrooms for the king and queen's six boys and seven girls. There was even a big bedroom for their dog.

"Don't worry," Jason said. "Their dog doesn't have accidents."

I took a picture of the castle. Jason wanted Mom to see what it looked like. "Take two pictures," he said. "We can give one to Cathy."

At home we sat on the front steps and shook the sand out of our shoes and socks. "We'll have an early dinner tonight," Dad said. "Do you boys still like pizza?"

"Sure," I said.

"I love it," Jason said.

"Me too," Cathy said.

"Then I know a great place for dinner," Dad told us. "It's a pizza place with old movies and video games."

"Great," I said. "I love video games."

Jason looked at me. Then he looked at Dad. "At home," he said, "you can call up the pizza place. And they'll bring the pizza to your house."

Dad laughed. "They do that here too. Would you like that?"

"Yes!" Jason shouted.

"Yes!" Cathy shouted.

I thought it was a rotten idea. But what could I say?

I packed our bags. Jason and Cathy played trucks on the living room floor. They used Lego blocks to build a garage.

"Matt," Dad said, "you can come with me. I need some help."

Dad and I drove to the pizza place. He ordered our pizza. Then we played video games while it was cooking.

I beat Dad most of the time. And he *didn't* let me win.

# CHAPTER NINE

We sat at the kitchen table and ate pizza. Cathy got an extra chair for Jason's toy dog, Willie. Willie had been playing trucks with them.

"Could Ben come in too?" Jason asked.

Dad looked at Ann. Ann winked at him.

So Ben came in for a little while. He even got a bite of pizza.

Then Jason and I brushed our teeth and got ready to go. Cathy stood and watched us. "I wish you didn't have to go," she said.

"She's kind of a brat," Jason whispered to me. "But she's an okay brat."

Cathy and Ann didn't come to the airport

with us. It was almost Cathy's bedtime. They walked out to the car with us.

"Bye-bye," Cathy said. She had to kiss Jason and me.

I don't like kissing much. But she was only four years old.

"Matt," Ann asked me, "would you do me a favor?"

"Sure." I was afraid she wanted to kiss me too.

"Would you take some pictures of the desert for me?" she asked. "You can bring them next time. I want to see what it's like."

"Sure," I said. "I'll get some good ones."

On the way to the airport Jason started to worry again. "What if something goes wrong?" he said. "What if we have to jump out of the plane?"

"Quit worrying," I said.

"I want answers," he said. "And a parachute."

"Don't be a baby," I told him.

"Hold it," Dad said. "Jason's not being a baby. He wants to know how things are. So he's asking questions."

"And I want real answers," Jason said. "Matt just tells me stuff so I'll shut up."

"What?" I said. That surprised me. It was true. But I didn't think he knew it.

"Matt's going to do better," Dad said. "And so am I. You want to know why you can't have a parachute?"

"Yes," Jason said.

"Parachutes were good in the old days," Dad said. "But they don't work with jet planes."

Jason leaned forward in his seat. "Why not?"

"Lots of reasons," Dad said. "For one thing, you can't open the door of the plane. They have to put extra air in the plane. It's like blowing up a balloon. Opening the door would be like putting a hole in the balloon."

"Oh," Jason said.

"Besides," Dad went on, "you don't need a parachute. Think about the plane you were on. Did it have only one motor?"

"It had two on each wing," Jason said.

"If one motor stops, the others can bring the plane in."

"Oh," Jason said.

Dad told us about how the planes were tested. And about the pilots. And about the safety equipment.

Jason yawned. "Dad," he said, "I changed my mind. I don't want a parachute."

At the airport we bought some sourdough bread. It was a present for Mom.

Then we walked to our gate. Jason laughed when he went through the metal check. "No dog chain," he said.

It was time to get on the plane. Dad hugged Jason. Then he hugged me. I'm a little old for hugging. But Dad didn't know that.

"It was great, Dad," I said. "And I'm not just saying it."

"It was great for me too," Dad said.

"Can I say something?" Jason asked.

"Sure," Dad said.

Jason looked over at me and then at Dad again. "You won't get mad?"

"We're family," Dad said. "You can say anything you want."

"Well," Jason said, "Ann's nice. And Cathy's okay." He stopped and looked over at me.

"Go ahead," Dad said. "What did you want to say?"

Jason looked down at the floor. "I wish you still lived at our house," he said quietly.

I liked hearing Jason say that. I'd been thinking the same thing. And I liked having it said out loud.

Dad picked up Jason and gave him another hug. "I know, son." Dad had tears in his eyes.

"Don't get all sad," Jason said. "We'll

come back and see you pretty soon."

Jason and I went down the ramp to our plane. He grabbed the ticket envelope out of my hand. Then he moved ahead of me. "We're in Row Eleven," he told the woman at the door. "Could I please get some cards?"

"Sure." The woman handed him a deck of cards.

"And my brother has an upset stomach," Jason told her. "Could you please bring him some 7-up when you have time?"

"I don't—" I started to say.

Jason gave me a push. "Jelly beans," he whispered.

We walked down the aisle. I saw that Jason was walking funny. "Did you hurt your leg?" I asked him.

"I'm fine," he said—too fast.

At Row Eleven, Jason took the seat by the window. Then he reached into his pants and brought out Willie. "Willie wanted to look out the window this trip," he said.

"You didn't have to hide him," I said.

"I didn't want everybody to see me with him," Jason said. "They'd think I was a little kid with his toy doggie."

I didn't answer that one.

Jason opened the deck of cards. "How about a game of Slap Jack?"

# ABOUT THE AUTHOR

P.J. Petersen was born in Santa Rosa, California, and grew up on a prune farm in Sonoma County. He attended Stanford University and holds the doctorate in English from the University of New Mexico.

He is the author of many books for young readers, including *Would You Settle for Improbable?* and *Nobody Else Can Walk It for You*, both American Library Association Best Books for Young Adults, and *Liars*, an American Bookseller Pick of the Lists.

Mr. Petersen lives with his family in Redding, California, and teaches at Shasta College.

# ABOUT THE ILLUSTRATOR

A graduate of the Pratt Institute, Anna DiVito is the author and illustrator of *Elephants on Ice* and has illustrated several other books for children. She lives with her husband in Unionville, New York.